Dear Little Wolf

This American edition published in 2002 by Carolrhoda Books, Inc.

Text copyright © 2000 by Ian Whybrow
Illustrations copyright © 2000 by Tony Ross

Published by arrangement with HarperCollins Publishers Ltd, London, England.
Originally published in English by HarperCollins Publishers Ltd under the title
LITTLE WOLF'S POSTBAG.

First Avenue Editions
An imprint of Lerner Publishing Group
241 First Avenue North
Minneapolis, MN 55401 U.S.A.

Website address: www.lernerbooks.com

Library of Congress Cataloging-in-Publication Data

Whybrow, Ian.
Dear Little Wolf / by Ian Whybrow ; illustrated by Tony Ross.
p. cm.
English edition published under title: Little Wolf's Postbag.
Summary: Little Wolf gets a job at Wolf Weekly magazine dispensing advice in
response to readers' letters, such as a skunk who wonders if she should change her
perfume.
ISBN: 0–87614–902–6 (pbk. : alk. paper)
[1. Wolves—Fiction. 2. Animals—Fiction. 3. Letters—Fiction. 4. Journalism—
Fiction.] I. Ross, Tony, ill. II. Title.
PZ7.W6225 De 2002
[E]—dc21
2001043291

Manufactured in the United States of America
2 3 4 5 6 – SB – 07 06 05 04

Dear Little Wolf

Ian Whybrow
Illustrated by Tony Ross

First Avenue Editions, Minneapolis

From the office of Wolf Weekly
POST OFFICE BOX 13
Frettnin Forest
Beastshire

Dear Mr. Little Wolf,

We have not met before, harrumph, but I feel I must write to you. At *Wolf Weekly* we keep getting letters from readers with problems, darn it. I am far too wolfish and snappish to write back, but I have reason to believe that you are just the brute beast for the job. Sit up straight and read on, and you will find out why.

This morning, a very small wolf cub entered my office wearing a mask. He had a water pistol and informed me that he would make the papers on my desk all crinkly unless I gave him a toffee apple. Grrrumph.

This small wolf cub was wearing his sailor suit inside out, so it was a simple matter to read the name tag on it. The name was one I think *you* know well: Smellybreff, your little brother. Pest! (Temper, you see. Snappishness. Can't help it.)

When I spoke to the small beast by his name, I suggested something that his parents might do if they found out that his hobby was

being a hold-up man. The result was that he howled his head off, threw himself on his back, and had a noisy tantrum. He claimed (while damaging my office floor with his head and heels) that it was all *your* fault. He claims (I quote): "Little is always making me be a robber plus mail his letters all the time. He says if I don't, he will put ketchup on my ted and eat him, then make me take a bath." And to prove it, he pulled out a wet and somewhat chewed envelope from his pocket.

Thanks to Smellybreff's dribble, the glue on the envelope had lost its grip. My curiosity was aroused and I was unable to resist opening the letter and reading it.

Drat and snap, now I feel too nagged and nitpicked to carry on with this. I think I had better go and shout at my secretary, then I shall feel better

Yours suddenly,

Peevish Wolfson the 3rd (Ed.)

Bah! Are you still there, Little Wolf?

Where was I? Ah, yes. Look, I hate praising, but bite me black and blue if that letter of yours wasn't a masterpiece! It was one you wrote to your parents who have their lair near the River Rover in Murkshire. You asked them to come and take your baby brother back, though not in so many words. You *suggested* that if they have their "darling little baby pet" tucked up with them this winter, they will save lots of cash on hot water bottles. I must admit that was brilliantly put. Crunch and gnash it! Sadly, however, to judge by my brief meeting with the ghastly Smellybreff, I suspect that they still prefer *you* to look after him.

You went on to mention in your letter that Smellybreff is in the habit of stealing your stamp collection and sticking it all over himself.

You tell your parents, "It might be a good idea if you sent him to a nice, far-off bunnyburger restaurant. There, he could be much happier everafter than staying with me in a big, drafty old house in Frettnin Forest."

Another very nice try. It showed imagination and—more importantly—*craftiness*!

Most of *Wolf Weekly*'s readers are just as spoiled, sad, and hopeless as your brother, grrrumph. They are always writing to the magazine with their problems. Nitwits! So I need an Agony Aunt who can write back with crafty and cunning ways to keep the moaners happy.

Hurry and let me know if *you* will take the job for a large salary.

I am, young sir, reluctantly yours,

Peevish Wolfson the 3rd (Ed.)

Not any more

HAUNTED HALL SCHOOL

FRETTNIN FOREST, BEASTSHIRE
HEADS: LITTLE WOLF AND YELLER WOLF ESQS
DEPUTY HEAD: SMELLYBREFF WOLF ESQ
CARETAKER: STUBBS CROW ARKSQWIRE

Dear Yeller,

You are a very funny tricker. Come on, that was *you* just saying you are Mister Editor of *Wolf Weekly* saying, "Have a job." You nearly made me fall for it 2, because the writing was all fancy, not like your normal loud and hilly words.

But I knew it was you at the end part, when you said, "for a large celery." Because you know I like crunchy snacks, but you did the spelling wrong, har, har!

So come on, fess up, who helped you?

Was it Stubbs, or Normus maybe?

Yours gotyoubackly,

Littly

P.S. What did you think of my frog-in-the-box? Did you like him jumping out and going squirt with pond water in your eye? Good, huh? I trained him 'specially for that.

MY ROOM
YORE HOWSE
FRETTNIN FORIST
BEESTYSHEAR

DEAR LBW,

TANKS A LOT FOR THE FROGGY, YUM YUM, TASTY. BY THE WAY, WHAT JOB? ALSO, WHAT IS AN EDITOR? DO YOU MEAN HEAD HITTER?

BECUZ I AM WUN OF THOSE, YOU CAN SEE THAT FROM MY TRICK RUBBER HAMMER ON A STRING THAT I SENT WIF THIS LETTER.

SO HEE HA HACK,
GOT YOU BACK!!

FROM YORE BEST FRIEND AND CUZ
WITH NO TAG-BACKS,

YELLER

P.S. I HAVE ASKED NORMUS AND
STUBBS, AND THEY SAID BEARS
AND CROWCHICKS DON'T DO
WRITY TRICKS BECUZ IT'S 2 HARD
FOR THEIR BRANES.

Not any more

HAUNTED HALL SCHOOL

FRETTNIN FOREST, BEASTSHIRE
HEADS: LITTLE WOLF AND YELLER WOLF ESQS
DEPUTY HEAD: SMELLYBREFF WOLF ESQ
CARETAKER: STUBBS CROW ARKSQWIRE

Dear Peevish Wolfson the somethingth,

I did not write back quick—sorry. I thought you were just my best friend and cuz Yeller doing wun of his tricks on me.

So, um, yes, if you want, I will be your letter answerer to your *Wolf Weekly* readers.

I like doing writing, but not being an Agony *Aunt*. Because I have a faymus dead uncle called Bigbad. Have you heard of him? He died of the jumping beanbangs and became ghost and star attraction at our school Haunted Hall. So, best if I can be an Agony *Nephew* instead.

Also, I like celery but will you pay me a large bag of gold instead? (I have lost all mine.)

Yours hintingly,

Mister Helpful (Get it?)

P.S. I am Little Wolf really, but ~~in~~ di~~zgizz~~ des~~goise~~ just pretending for your Problem Page in Wolf Weekly.

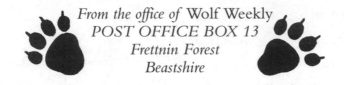

From the office of Wolf Weekly
POST OFFICE BOX 13
Frettnin Forest
Beastshire

Dear Little Wolf,

Thank you (achh, I hate having to say that). Anyway, what I just said for agreeing to work for me. All those little pests moaning on and on were starting to set my teeth on edge. But you have obviously had plenty of practice in dealing with moaners like your baby brother and your splendid arch-criminal uncle, Bigbad Wolf.

It pains me to admit it, bah, but I like the name Mister Helpful. It is a fine disguising name, or, as they say in French, a *nom de plume*.

Now you had better make a start at agony answering. I am enclosing a hopeless letter from a fearfully sad young wolverine. You are to

deal with it. This is a test. If you succeed, you shall have gold. If you fail, I shall send you a tape recording of me going "Bah, young cubs today are useless! Not like me, when I was a young chaser. They always let you down!" Et cetera, et cetera.

Yours doubtingly,

Peevish Wolfson the 3rd (Ed.)

enc.

Ma Belle Maison Splendide
Dogood Way
Near Windy Ridge
Beastshire

Dear Wolf Weekly,

I love your magazine, especially fur and fitness tips. But what tips can you give for cubsitting? I am starting my first job as a

sitter soon, and I fear baby wolfies can be difficult. Is loving care enough?

Yours anxiously,

Prudence Wolf (Miss)

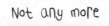

HAUNTED HALL SCHOOL

FRETTNIN FOREST, BEASTSHIRE
HEADS: LITTLE WOLF AND YELLER WOLF ESQS
DEPUTY HEAD: SMELLYBREFF WOLF ESQ
CARETAKER: STUBBS CROW ARKSQWIRE

Dear Mister Wolfson,

You remind me of Uncle, making me do tests and saying Or Else. How do you spell nat? Is there a "g" in it? (Cannot find room for wun.)

Any gold coming my way, hint, hint?

Yours testedly,

L. Bad Wolf the wunth

19

Will this answer do?

From the Sharp Pencil of Mister Helpful ~
Wolf Weekly's Agony Nephew

Dear Miss Prudence,

Too bad about you having such simple dimple ideas. But never mind. I have done you tips in a poem so even a ~~ngt ngat~~ nat could learn them just by humming them over and over.

Wolfcubsitting for Beginners

If baby is a problem
And you don't know what to do,
Give him something fun to play with,
Like a nice big pot of glue.

Tip 2 for the baby wolfie is,
If he goes wah wah,
Take him out for pizza,
Or let him drive your car.

If wolfie keeps on crying,
Sit down in your chair,
Give him a pair of scissors
And let him cut your hair.

If baby wets his nickers,
The best thing you can do,
So he will not get all upset
Is wet your nickers 2.

Wun last tip for beginners is,
(You will find this helps a lot),
Let the baby watch T.V.,
Then you can have a nice long
zizz in his cot.

Yours tippingly,

Mr. Helpful

Dear L.W.,

You are hired. You know how much it irritates me to say excellent, so I won't. I will say *Tish*, *Tosh* and *Grrrumph* instead, and you will just have to work out what I really think and accept this medium-size bag of gold. Keep doing work of this quality and I shall be forced, rrreluctantly, to send you an even larger one.

Now hurry up, write yourself an announcement so that readers will be expecting you. Come on, get on with it. I shall print it in the Variety Page.

I remain yours hatefully with a capital Harrr,

Peevish Wolfson the 3rd (Ed.)

BOTTLED GHOST OF BIGBAD WOLF STILL MISSING: FOX SUSPECTED.

... AND THERE IS still no sign of the missing ghost of ex-Criminal and Terror, Bigbad Wolf. He was formerly headmaster of Frettnin Forest's Cunning College, and later, School Spirit and Resident Horror of Haunted Hall. Our reporter has learned that the bottle in which he made his grave on account of its label, "Powerful Spirit," has been stolen. The number 1 suspect remains Mister Twister, Foxy Crook and Master of Disguises, but his whereabouts are unknown.

BEAVER ARRESTED FOR SWEARING

LAST NIGHT Frettnin Forest police were questioning a beaver who was very rude after a sliding incident on the banks of the River Riggly. Asked by Officer Thick where he lived, he answered, "A big dam."

WOLVES MAKE A MEAL OF BUNNY WANDERERS IN CUP SEMIFINAL

IT WAS SPILLS, thrills, and cooking skills all the way at the Howl Lane soccer field today. The home team just gobbled up the opposition.

In just 35 seconds, the Wanderers were in the net. They were in the pot after just one minute, and served up with carrots and boiled potatoes well before halftime. With the entire opposition off the field, the Wolves were able to shoot at will, but they could only be bothered to score three goals each.

Commenting later, team coach Terry Grab said: "Give credit to the Wanderers. They had some very tasty and seasoned players. I thought their goalie was really spicy."

Final score:
Wolves 99
Wanderers 0

CRICKET NEWS
Chirrup, chirrup, chirrup.

CALLING ALL READERS!

Arrrroooo!

CALLING ALL READERS of Wolf Weekly Weekly. Guess who is going to be your new problem page Agony Nephew? Me. I am Little Wolf really, but you must pretend not knowing and say "Dear Mister Helpful" if you want to get a reply printed all fancily in this faymus mag. Because Mister Helpful is my nom de prune (French).

So come on, what's up with you? write quick.

The Hole
Under Bush 1276040
Frettnin Forest
Beastshire

Dear Little—woops, sorry, I mean Mister Helpful,

I feel starving all the time, even just after dinner and snacks. What can I do about it?

Yours probingly,

Antony Anteater

Dear Antony,

Having trouble getting food through? Y not get a bigger hanky and try doing xtra hard honks in it?

If your nose is still blocked up, try a pipe cleaner. Also, here is a good tip. If your friends say "Let's go out to the anthill and have a good blowout," that means suck really, so careful not to go in reverse.

Yours *bong appetitely* (meaning enjoy your grubs, French),

Monsieur Helpful

P.S. You could try picking more. But not at parties (a bit rude, hem, hem).

The Compost Heap
Up the messy end of Bodger Badger's garden
The Set
Spooke
Grimshire

Dear Mister Helpful,

My dad makes me feel really, really small all the time. He says things like, "You will never make anything of yourself, only a crunchy snack."

My dream is to be the best xylophone player in Beastshire. I have the arms and legs for it, don't you think?

Please be encouraging.

Yours crawlily,

Milly Pede

Dear Milly,

About being a crunchy snack or a xylophone player. That is a hard wun. Your best thing is, go over to my Dad's lair and say, "Hello Mr. Wolf, Mr. Helpful says can I play 'Take Me Out to the Ballgame' on your toothies?" You will soon find out which wun you are best at.

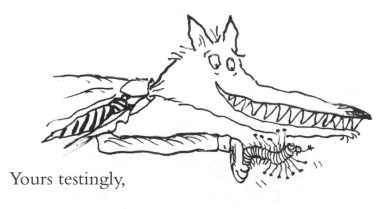

Yours testingly,

L. Wolf, Mister Helpful

The Lair
Lonesome Mountain
River Rover North
Murkshire

Dear Son,

I know it is you being Mister Helpful. You cannot fool me—I am your mother. Leave it to you to ruin our family reputation for wicked selfishness and badness. You have always been a bit of a goodie 4-paws. I s'pect your Uncle Bigbad's ghost is turning over in his bottle if he knows what you are up to.

But, did you send a pesky millipede around to annoy your father? **Well done!** That was more wolfish. It made him go raving mad with a fangache. He had to go to the dentist, and do you know what he found? A

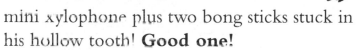

mini xylophone plus two bong sticks stuck in his hollow tooth! **Good one!**

So your reward is that you can look after our darling baby pet Smellybreff for a bit longer. Remember, give him everything he whines for. It is the only way.

Love,

Mom

P.S. Make sure this pic gets in your fancy mag, I had it taken 'specially.

Bodger Badger's Garage
The Set
Spooke
Grimshire

Hello,

The thing is, oooh, arr,
Oy was rootin' around
at the top of my garden
last week, when Oy
heard be-ootiful music
come a-tinklin' from
moy compost heap.
Blow me down if it
wasn't a teeny little
bug a-playin' on one
of them there
xylophone things.
Fantarstic it was.

Yippee! Oy am a bit slow on the uptake, but Oy have just had a fantarstic idea! Oy reckon Oy shall make a fortune chargin' folks to come and have a listen! Then Oy shall buy meself a chicken farm and give up garage work. Now, moy problem is, Oy can't make up me moind, should Oy start counting me chickens yet?

Yours oooh–arrly,

Bodger Badger

Dear Bodger,

Ummm, no, probly not, sorry. My dad has gobbled your music player.

But if you are up for a nice change from garage work, I will give a tip 2 you. Take your glasses off 1st. Glue some feathers on your wrenches, then hold out some corn saying, "Here chicky chicky."

Yours nevermindly,

Mr. Helpful

Dear Mister Help,

I am a teenage leopard but I have no spots at all. I feel so ashamed. What can I do?

Yours embarrassedly,

Whizz Fleetfoot (age 2, but don't forget to times by 7, OK?)

Dear Whizzy,

Keep eating lots of greasy food plus sweets, chips, and all stuff like that. If still no spots, find a hole in a wall and move in. Put up a notice outside saying HANSUM LARGE WEASUL, then everyone will go, "Gosh, has he got big mussuls for a rodent."

Yours adequately,

Mister Helpful

Dear Mr. Hurtful,

Sometimes I get so lonely. Would it help if I changed my perfume? Please be frank. My best friends will not tell me.

Yours defensively,

Irma Skunk

SMELL THIS SAMPLE

P.S. I am spraying you a small sample on this letter.

Dear Irma,

Pew! Dank you for da dample
dat you dent. How long before
I can take the peg off my
doze?!!

I hab passed your
letter on to Wiffer
Warthog, The Hogwallow,
Muckheap on Sea.

You 2 will be a happy couple together, I bet.
Plead do not bodder to wride and dank me.

Yours gassedly,

Mister Fainting

Watcher Matey,

 My old Cock Sparrow and me are not feelin' our normal chirpy selves. We have problems with our new chicky, just 2 weeks out of his egg.

I am not sayin' he is fat. But put it this way: feedin' him his grubs is like tryin' to load a cement mixer with a teaspoon. Also, he takes up all the nest already. Plus, his voice is a bit funny. He never seems to say "cheep" or "tweet" like our other babies dun. He just seems to get the hiccups sort of. We are worried about what he will be when he grows up.

Yours down in the beakly,

Mrs. Hazel Edge-Sparrow

Dear Mrs. Sparrow,

Never mind if your fat chicky is a hopeless flier and tweeter. Just teach him to count up to 12 and pop him in a clock. (Must be Swiss, and do not forget to put him on a bit of elastic.) Then he will have a nice job for life.

Yours guessingly,

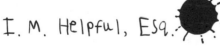

I. M. Helpful, Esq.

P.S. Does he go "cook" and "oo" a lot? I bet he does.

The Filthy Mantled Pool
Yellowsmoke Swamplands

Dear Mister H,

Let me just yelp that I need some help,
And I need it in a hurry.

I ain't no liar, my throat's on fire,
And my mouth is kinda furry.

Get me off the hook, come and take a look,
Cuz you're a real nice kind of chappy.

Pop along today with a soothing spray,
And Mister, make it snappy.

Yours saying Ahly,

Al R. Gator

Dear Al,

Have we met before? Is your middle name Rap? I think it is, and wun time you swallowed a small cub listening to his Walkwolf, didn't you? Anyway, thank you for your letter. It was quite catchy. Sad about your sore throat. In a way, hem, hem.

I am a bit 2 busy to jump in your mouth today. Your best bet is to hang a very large sign saying OPTICIAN on your snout. If you are very lucky, maybe a nearsighted doctor will pop in for an eye test.

Or if you know any piglets with water pistols, maybe you could throw them a bottle of mouthwash and say, "Hey, you smellies, I bet you can't squirt the little dangly thing up the dark end of my trap with this."

Tempting, huh?

Yours soothingly,

Mister Helpful

THE PILE OF LEAVES
THE HEDGE
NEAR THE BIG BEECH TREE THAT GOES EEK
IN A STRONG WIND

DEAR MISTER HELPFUL,

When I was younger, I had lots of fun playing soccer, but not any more. I cannot even touch my toes. These days I am feeling so low down, I do not know what has come over me. Can you recommend a pick-me-up?

Yours flatly,

SPIKY HEDGEHOG

Dear Spiky,

You say you do not know what has come over you. Did it go *Brrrm Brrm Beep*? If it did, your best pick-me-up is probly a shovel. Or, if not, Y not tumble dry yourself? Jump in the dryer wunce a week, and that way you will soon be rolling over and over like washing. After, if you are still lousy at kicking and heading, never mind, you can be the soccer ball.

Yours sportingly,

Mister Helpful

Dear Mister,

I do not know how I shall ever hold my chin above water again. My tail just fell off. What shall I do? I feel so unattractive.

Yours pointlessly,

Newton Newt

Dear Newton,

Newts' tails are all damp and horrible anyway.

My best advice is, forget it. Just do a hop and a skip, saying:

I am so luckee,
My tail fell off todee,
So now there is less of me,
To get all cold and clammy!
Hip hip hoorah times 3!

P.S. You can buy blue stuff at the store for sticking up posters and tails. It is called Newtack. But as I say, y bother?

49

The Swanky House
Fancy End
2, Pepper Lane
Dark Hills
Beastshire

Dear Mister Helpful,

On behalf of all the dear creatures of Frettnin Forest who have benefited recently by your magnificent advice, allow me to express our sincere gratitude.

Please come over to my enormous mansion and collect a luxury basket of succulent food. Although I am of huge richness, I am but a weak and helpless widow.

I am sending you a picture of me in my old lady's nightie and glasses and everything. Sad to say, therefore, I will be unable to leave my bed and hand it to you personally. Instead, I  shall leave it for you in a safe place in a big black sack at the bottom of a deep pit in my garden.

Feel free to pop down and collect it any time. Can you advise me when to expect you?

Your devoted fan,

Miss ER Wittert

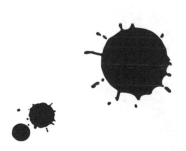

From the Sharp Pencil of Mister Helpful ~
Wolf Weekly's *Agony Nephew*

Dear Mister Twister,

What a twisty letter you sended. I know you are not really Miss ER Wittert. That was just a mixup of your real name, right?

But I knew it was you. Because clue number 1 was your foxy paper made me sneeze by its peppery smell.

Plus, clue 2 was your tail coming out peepingly from under the bedclothes in the photo.

Plus, clue 3: you left a red whisker sticking to the stamp.

You ask if I can advise you. The answer is yes, here I go. Can you see my pic A of a piece of string?

Now can you see pic B?

It is the same string as pic A only with knots in it. Good, because now you must copy pic B—ready, steddy, go.

Now you are knotted. Har, har.

Yours unfooledly,

Guess who?

Bathing Towel House
Scouting Lane
Roaring River
Murkshire
CUB 3RD

Dear Mr. Helpful,

I am trying to locate a wolf cub by the name of Little. He is an honorary member of my pack, the 3rd Murkshire. Can you assist me, please?

I met him last summer in Beastshire, on the shores of Lake Lemming in Frettnin Forest, where I had taken my Cub Scout troop on a camping trip. He stayed with us for quite a while and achieved a great deal for a small furry animal.

He gained his Navigator and Explorer badges, and he took particular pride in the special Cub Scout Adventure Award (1st Class) with certificate and badge that we awarded him. And we were over the moon to have him in our  pack. Because, as I said to him then, "Sonny jim, you have made our visit to Frettnin Forest something special. You are the first real wolf cub we have met."

My patrol leaders, Sanjay and Dave, never stop talking about Little Wolf. He was such a cheerful young chappy. This year, we are looking forward to a jamboree, a big gathering of all the Cub Scouts in Murkshire and Beastshire. We have picked the perfect spot for it—Spring Valley, just by the bend in the Spring River, Southeast of Lonesome Woods. Smashing tent country!

My problem is this. There has been a lot of talk lately that Spring Valley is haunted. They say that ever since he went bang, the ghost of the dreadful Bigbad Wolf wanders around in the woods and forests, shocking innocent wanderers with his great, big, horrible red eyes and his great, big, horrible yellow teeth. All nonsense, I dare say. But because of the rumors, I can hardly get enough cubs together to fill one tent, let alone make up a proper Jamboree. Very disappointing.

You would be doing a very good deed if you could put me in touch with Little Wolf. If he (and perhaps some of his friends) would join us, I feel certain that it would encourage some of the faint-hearted chappies to change their minds and come camping!

Yours DYB DOB DYBly

Jim Toggle (Akela)

From the Sharp Pencil of Mister Helpful ~
Wolf Weekly's *Agony Nephew*

Dear Mr. Toggle,

Lucky you wrote to me, because I know all about L. Wolf Esq. Also about his cheerfulness and young chappyness, thank you, hem, hem. I let him read your letter, and he has sent you 1 back.

Yours gooddeedly,

Mister Helpful

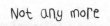
HAUNTED HALL SCHOOL

FRETTNIN FOREST, BEASTSHIRE
HEADS: LITTLE WOLF AND YELLER WOLF ESQS
DEPUTY HEAD: SMELLYBREFF WOLF ESQ
CARETAKER: STUBBS CROW ARKSQWIRE

Dear Akela,

Arrroooo! from me (Little Wolf) to you. Also to Sanjay and Dave.

Mr. Helpful says you want to get some cubs together for camping near Lonesome Woods. Good, because camping used to be my worst thing, but now I love it, kiss, kiss.

I will bring my best friend and cuz Yeller. He is loudest with the best ideas, plus a fine tricker. Next is Stubbs, only a crowchick, but he has a clever beak plus

he does good loop the loops. Normus Bear is my newest chum. He does not fly (no wings), and his ideas are silly but he is already a cub, also tuff, and likes daring deeds. They all say ARRRRROOOOOOOOOO! to jamborees!

Plus, do not fret and frown, we have got a plan for getting you lots more to be in your pack. So bring plenty of tents. See you in Spring Valley.

Yours surprisingly,

L. B. W.

P.S. I will have to bring my baby bro, Smellybreff. He is OK in a way, but best not teach him lighting fires, all right?

P.P.S. Me, Yeller, Stubbs, Normus, and Smells have made a detective pack called *Yelloweyes Detective Agency*. If you need anything detected, just let us know.

CALLING ALL READERS!

Arrrrooooooo!

Stop being wurrid. Come and be in a cubscout pack instead with Little Wolf, Smellybreff, Yeller, Stubbs, and Normus and do jamboreeing in Spring Valley.

We will have campfires, singsongs, games, badgework, chocklit bars, adventures, alphabetti spaghetti, and SPESHLY humshuss and scrumshuss bakebeans, hmm yessss!!

I *was* Mister Helpful, but I am fed up with being Agony Nephew now. It gives you an armache and not enuff muckabouting. Plus, Mr. Peevish Wolfson says:

So change WURRY to HURRY and
LET'S JAMBOREEEEEE!

Arrrrrrrrooooooo!

Yours ridingalongonthecrestofawavely,

Little Wolf